BEASTQUEST

THE DARK REALM

↦ BOOK FOURTEEN ↤

SKOR
THE WINGED STALLION

ADAM BLADE

ILLUSTRATED BY EZRA TUCKER

SCHOLASTIC INC.

New York   Toronto   London   Auckland
Sydney   Mexico City   New Delhi   Hong Kong

With special thanks to Michael Ford

To Connor Kennedy

No part of this work may be reproduced, stored in a retrieval system, or transmitted in any form or by any means, electronic, mechanical, photocopying, recording, or otherwise, without written permission of the publisher. For information regarding permission, write to Working Partners Ltd., Stanley House, St. Chad's Place, London WC1X 9HH, United Kingdom.

ISBN: 978-0-545-20032-5

Beast Quest series created by Working Partners Ltd., London. BEAST QUEST is a trademark of Working Partners Ltd.

Text © 2008 by Working Partners Ltd. All rights reserved.
Cover illustration © 2008 by David Wyatt
Illustrations © 2010 by Scholastic Inc.

Published by Scholastic Inc., 557 Broadway, New York, NY 10012, by arrangement with Working Partners Ltd. SCHOLASTIC, LITTLE APPLE, and associated logos are trademarks and/or registered trademarks of Scholastic Inc.

12 11 10 9 8 7 6 5 4 3 2 1   10 11 12 13 14 15/0

Designed by Tim Hall
Printed in the U.S.A.   40
First printing, January 2010

Welcome. You stand on the edge of darkness, at the gates of an awful land. This place is Gorgonia, the Dark Realm, where the sky is red, the water black, and Malvel rules. Tom and Elenna — your hero and his companion — must travel here to complete the next Beast Quest.

Gorgonia is home to six most deadly Beasts — Minotaur, Winged Stallion, Sea Monster, Gorgonian Hound, Mighty Mammoth, and Scorpion Man. Nothing can prepare Tom and Elenna for what they are about to face. Their past victories mean little. Only strong hearts and determination will save them now.

Dare you follow Tom's path once more? I advise you to turn back. Heroes can be stubborn and adventures may beckon, but if you decide to stay with Tom, you must be brave and fearless. Anything less will mean certain doom.

Watch your step. . . .

Kerlo the Gatekeeper

HALLAM PEERED THROUGH THE GLOOM. HE hardly dared take another step. Shafts of light danced across the rain forest floor as the canopy of leaves swayed above. Who knew what creatures lurked behind the thick trunks, or under the giant fern leaves?

He moved slowly over the mossy ground. Noises echoed among the trees — shrill shrieks and low cackles. This place was nothing like the woodland where he and the other Gorgonian rebels used to hide. There, the worst thing a traveler might come across would be a wild boar.

But the forest wasn't safe now. Not since the Dark Wizard Malvel had closed his net across Gorgonia. His ruthless armies scoured the land for rebels, burning the villages of innocent people. There were Beasts, too. Hallam shuddered as he remembered the deaths of his two comrades. Torgor the Minotaur had torn them limb from limb.

Hallam plunged on, flashing glances in the direction of every sound. His sweat-soaked clothes clung to his body. A vine brushed against the back of his neck. He reached up to brush it away, but it wriggled beneath his touch. A snake!

"Urgh!" Hallam cried out, falling backward.

The snake landed a foot away and drew itself into a coil, hissing. Its scales were a glistening yellow, its eyes bloodred. Hallam lay on the ground, frozen with fear. The snake fixed him with its eyes, its forked tongue flickering in and out, its head swaying, before it uncoiled and slithered away.

Hallam climbed to his feet, brushing wet leaves from his tunic. He pushed on through the trees. *You'll have to be more careful!* he told himself. *Where there's* one *snake . . .*

Hallam was so busy watching the trees that he didn't notice where he was putting his feet. The next moment, he was sliding down a massive slope. The plants on either side of him were a blur as he skidded past. And then he saw what waited at the bottom.

A pit of writhing vipers!

He scrambled to slow himself, but the mud was too slippery. Vines broke off in his hand. He jammed his heels into the ground. A hair's width from the deadly mass of snakes, he stopped.

The blood thumped in his head, louder than the calls of the birds above.

Trembling, Hallam began to push himself back up the slope.

You fool! he thought. *Malvel's soldiers will find you if you don't watch your step!*

He didn't take his eyes off the snakes. He wanted to get out of the rain forest as quickly as possible.

His back came up against a tree trunk. He gripped the bark with his palms, and then felt something soft, like . . . feathers. Hot breath misted the air above his head.

Hallam spun around.

A horse's head pushed through the branches above him. But this was no ordinary horse. It towered over Hallam and stared down at him. *A Beast!* Hallam gasped for breath, his stomach turning over with fear. The creature's lips drew back, revealing a set of menacing teeth, dripping with strings of saliva.

Hallam fell to his knees at the Beast's golden hooves. Huge wings opened from the stallion's body, lifting it above the ground. The creature swayed among the trees, his powerful legs kicking, then he threw back his head and screeched as Hallam cowered on the ground. Silver sparks flashed from the Beast's eyes, lighting up the glossy leaves of the jungle, before the fearsome teeth began to close in. . . .

CHAPTER ONE

A VISION IN THE WATER

"WE HAVE TO CLEAN YOU UP," SAID ELENNA.

Tom and his friend stood beside the river that wound through the dusty Gorgonian plains. It was nothing like the clear streams of Avantia. Here the water was brown and sludgy. Every so often, bubbles escaped to the surface, bursting and filling the air with rotten-smelling yellow gas.

Elenna dabbed the gashes on Tom's arm where Torgor the Minotaur's mighty ax had wounded him. The enchanted feather in Tom's shield, given to him by Epos the Winged Flame, had run out of power before it could heal all of his injuries. It had been Tom's toughest fight yet, but he had managed to free Tagus the Night Horse from the clutches of Torgor. Now the good Beast was safely back in Avantia, away from Malvel's evil.

"Do you think the herbs will work?" asked Tom.

Elenna smiled as she ground the herbs Tom's aunt had given them. With some of the water from her flask, the mixture became a thick paste. Silver the wolf watched as she worked the paste into Tom's wounds.

"Thank you," Tom said. He didn't know how he would have survived without Elenna on his Quests.

The pain in his arm began to ebb away.

"It's working!" he said.

The memories of the battle would take longer to fade, though. Torgor was more deadly than any Beast they had faced before. If there were other such creatures in Gorgonia, Tom knew he would need all his strength and courage to defeat them.

Elenna was bandaging the last of the linen dressings over Tom's gashes when Silver leaped to his feet and began pacing along the riverbank, barking wildly at the water.

Tom's horse, Storm, stamped his hooves and shook his mane, then backed away from the river's edge.

"What's gotten into Storm and Silver?" asked Elenna.

"Something's spooking them," said Tom. He peered into the water. The current seemed to have stopped. Silver let out a high-pitched whine. A pool rippled in the middle of the water.

The two friends gazed into the river as the patterns there shifted. Gradually they could see the lines of a mouth, then a nose, and then two eyes. Ripples like long white hairs framed the image. The mouth moved in little waves.

Elenna gasped.

"Aduro!" said Tom.

It was their friend the good wizard of Avantia.

"Greetings, Tom and Elenna," the vision in the water said.

"Greetings," they replied.

"Once again, congratulations on overcoming Torgor," said Aduro. "Tagus sends his thanks from Avantia."

Elenna squeezed Tom's arm, and Aduro continued.

"But, as you know, my magic is weak here in Gorgonia — the gateway between worlds saps my energy. I don't have the power to stay with you long."

"Tell us, Aduro," said Tom, "what is our next Quest?"

"You must track down a new Beast," said Aduro. "Its name is Skor."

Tom shot Elenna a look. She shrugged, looking mystified.

Aduro's face began to soften at the edges, and

his words became distant. His magic was fading. "Beware," he whispered. "I give you a final warning: Danger will come from both earth and air. Remember, earth and air . . ."

The face melted back into the water.

"He's gone!" said Tom.

"What is Skor?" said Elenna. "How can it be a danger by earth and air?"

"I don't know," said Tom, "but we have to find out. We already know that Epos is in danger." After the defeat of Torgor, the flame bird's feather in Tom's shield had begun to glow, calling for their help.

Tom picked up his shield, swung it onto his back, and tightened his magic belt around his waist. Already, one of the slots contained the ruby jewel he had captured from Torgor, so he now had the ability to understand what the Beasts were thinking. But there were five slots still to fill. He wondered what new powers he would gain on this Quest.

"Let's see where we have to head next," said Tom.

Elenna opened the bag on Storm's saddle and pulled out the map given to them by Malvel. Unlike the enchanted parchment that had guided them in Avantia, this map was scrawled on rotten animal hide. Tom shuddered as he helped Elenna unroll the greasy yellow surface.

"Look!" said Elenna. "A path . . ."

The stench of the map was overpowering, and Tom held his breath as he leaned in closer. A green line became clear against the discolored surface. It marked a route from their present location on the plains. The line snaked around steep rocky gullies and ravines, and ended in a place of tall trees many miles away. They could see the figure of a tiny phoenix hidden within the trees.

"It's a rain forest! And there's Epos," said Tom.

"It looks dangerous," said Elenna.

Tom put his hand on her shoulder. "We've overcome thirteen Beasts already," he said. "We can do it if we work together."

"We don't even know if we can trust the map," said Elenna. "Malvel may be leading us to our deaths."

Tom nodded. "Whatever Malvel throws at us, we'll be prepared," he said, rolling up the map. He gazed beyond the river. "Epos needs our help. We won't fail."

CHAPTER TWO

TOWARD DANGER

STORM GALLOPED ACROSS THE DUSTY PLAINS, Silver bounding tirelessly by his side. Gorgonia's sun was hidden behind thick banks of swirling red clouds, and the gloom seemed to press down upon them, ready to swallow them up. The stallion's hooves struggled to find a grip on the crumbling soil, and twice he nearly fell. But Tom gripped Storm's flanks with his thighs, watching the terrain to avoid any loose rocks.

"Gorgonia makes me miss Avantia," said Elenna, over the pounding of Storm's hooves. "This feels like a land of —"

"Death?" said Tom.

Elenna shivered, as though a chill had run down her spine. There was no sign of life anywhere in Malvel's kingdom, and the stench of decay filled the air. It was as though the Dark Wizard himself was following them, breathing down their necks.

Something appeared on the horizon. Tom felt his heartbeat quicken. He tightened Storm's reins and slowed the stallion to a canter, and he felt Elenna grip his waist. But his pulse steadied as he realized it was only a dead tree.

It looked like a skeletal hand, reaching upward from the earth. The branches were leafless and decayed, and a huge vulture with patchy brown feathers perched there. As they trotted past, it swiveled its bald head and fixed them with a black stare. Tom could feel the scavenger's eyes watching them as they trotted away. Silver howled nervously.

"One of Malvel's spies?" Elenna whispered into Tom's ear.

"Who knows?" Tom said, trying not to shudder.

Soon they came to a small watering hole, which looked a little cleaner than the river. Tom and Elenna dismounted and took out their flasks, while Storm trotted over to the water's edge. He bowed his head to drink, then sniffed and neighed. Silver flattened his ears and growled.

"What's the matter, boy?" asked Elenna. Then she spotted something on the far side of the pool. "Urgh!" she cried, and pointed.

A white rib cage, picked clean of flesh, broke the surface of the water. Flies buzzed over it.

"What do you think it once was?" asked Elenna.

"I don't know," Tom replied, "but this water isn't safe. I'd rather be parched than poisoned."

Remounting Storm, Tom stroked his mane. "I

know you're thirsty, boy, but we've got to keep going."

Storm threw back his head and shook his mane, letting out a whinny. Tom dug in his heels, and the stallion shot forward once again. They made good speed across the plains. Ahead, the air shimmered with heat, and Tom could see nothing but pale brown earth, with an occasional spiky gorse bush. But a tingle in his stomach told him something was wrong.

After a while, the gorse bushes became thicker, and Tom had to keep his eyes on the ground to steer Storm through safely. He was worried. Was Malvel driving them into the middle of nowhere, where starvation and thirst would wear them down?

"Look out!" yelled Elenna.

Tom saw a cliff edge right in front of them. He pulled back on Storm's reins as hard as he could, and the horse let out a terrified neigh, tossing his head in panic, his hooves skidding toward the edge of the drop and throwing up clouds of dust.

"He doesn't have enough time to stop!" Tom shouted.

They were going over the edge!

↦ Chapter Three ↤

INTO THE GORGE

Storm's body arched under the saddle as he reared back, his front hooves wheeling in the air. Pebbles clattered down into the gulley below, and the edge of the cliff started to crumble. Elenna's fingers dug into Tom's sides and he felt his weight shift backward. He lost his hold on the reins. But somehow Storm's hooves found a grip. Tom heard a thump on the ground behind him, and when he looked, he could see that Elenna had fallen to safety.

But twisting around in the saddle made Tom lose his balance. He tried to grab Storm's mane to steady himself, but it was too late. He was falling!

The empty valley opened up below him, as rocks and pebbles scattered. His body knocked into the side of the cliff . . . then pain jolted through his ankle. He was suspended in the air, his arms dangling. His cheeks were grazed by the rough stones, but he was alive.

"Storm's stirrup!" Tom shouted. "It saved me!"

But he hardly dared to move. Only his foot, caught in the stirrup, stopped him from hurtling into the depths of the canyon. Even the magic token in his shield that protected him from falls might not be able to help him in a ravine as deep as this.

Elenna poked her head over the cliff edge. "Hold on!" she shouted.

"I'm not going anywhere," said Tom.

Then he heard her talk to Storm. "That's right, boy, slowly," she coaxed, encouraging the stallion to walk away from the cliff edge and pull Tom back up to solid ground. But he knew they would

have to go slowly — or his foot might slip loose of the stirrup.

Tom felt himself being gradually heaved up the cliff. As soon as he felt Storm approach solid ground, he twisted around carefully and used his arms to scramble to safety. He pulled his foot from the stirrup and lay back on the dusty earth, gasping with relief. Silver padded over to lick his face, and Tom reached out a hand to pat the wolf's neck.

"Thank you, Elenna!" he said. Storm whinnied. "And you, Storm," Tom added.

The stallion's flank was slick with sweat and his legs were trembling.

Elenna stroked his nose. "There, there, boy, it's all right." Then she stepped over to gaze down into the ravine. "Do you think anything lives down there?" she asked, her voice echoing off the rocks below.

"I don't know, but we must get across to rescue Epos," said Tom. He pointed to the trees on the other side of the gorge. "That has to be the rain forest."

"But how?" said Elenna. "It's too far to jump, even on Storm's back."

The gorge was as wide as ten houses.

Tom scanned the distance with his keen sight, one of the powers he had won during his Quest to find the golden armor. He spotted something dark arcing across the gorge. A bridge! It looked narrow and flimsy, but it was the only choice they had.

"I can see a bridge," he said. "We can cross there."

He swung himself back into Storm's saddle and offered a hand to Elenna. She was pale.

"What's the matter?" Tom asked.

His friend bowed her head in shame. "It's just that, ever since I was young, I've been terrified of heights."

Tom climbed down from Storm and placed both hands on her shoulders. "We've battled thirteen Beasts and won," he said. "I know you have the strength to meet this challenge."

Elenna looked up, and Tom saw her face had changed. Fierce determination shone in her eyes.

"Let's do it," she said.

The two of them scrambled into Storm's saddle. Then Tom drove his horse in a gallop toward the bridge. Silver's fur flattened as he bounded beside them. As the bridge drew near, Tom slowed Storm to a canter.

"It doesn't look very safe," Elenna said.

Tom felt doubt tighten his throat. The bridge that spanned the gorge looked ancient. The rope rails were thin and frayed, and the wooden planks were black with age. Then he remembered the gift given to him by the golden chain mail — strength of heart.

"It's the only way for both of us to cross," he said. "But Storm is too heavy — the bridge won't hold him. He'll have to stay here with Silver."

"Yes," said Elenna. Tom felt her twist in the saddle. "Where *is* Silver?"

Tom spun around. The wolf was nowhere to be seen.

"Silver!" shouted Elenna. "Where are you?"

A howl sounded back, from behind a nearby cluster of boulders. They dashed in the direction of the noise and found Silver. He was sniffing a bush loaded with bright red berries.

"Food!" said Elenna. "Clever boy, Silver." She ruffled his fur, then started to pick the fruit.

Tom joined her. It had been so long since they last ate. Tom stuffed the juicy berries into his mouth until the sticky sweet juice dribbled down his chin.

"They taste so good." Elenna laughed, licking her fingers. "Who would have thought something so delicious could grow in Gorgonia?"

Tom stopped. Elenna was right. The berries tasted *too* good. He spat out his mouthful, and stared at his friend. Elenna was blurring in front of him. Tom held his hand up to his face — his fingers became hazy around the edges. He staggered sideways.

"The berries!" he said. "They're poisonous!"

It was another of Malvel's evil tricks.

Elenna stumbled toward him. "Something is wrong with my eyes! What shall we do?" she asked.

Tom pointed shakily to the gorge. "We have to get across the bridge — while we still can. We can't let Malvel end our Quest before it's really begun!"

Holding on to each other, they walked unsteadily toward the edge of the cliff. Storm came to their side.

"You'll have to stay here," said Tom, unhooking his shield from the stallion's saddle and patting his head.

Silver lifted his nose and licked Elenna's hand.

"You too, Silver," she said.

The wolf dropped back, letting out a worried whine.

Tom edged toward the bridge. It was so narrow and he felt so unsteady on his feet.

"We'll have to go one at a time," he said. "Let me lead the way."

A strong wind had picked up, gusting along the gorge. The rope bridge swayed and creaked. Tom shuddered. None of his special powers could help him now. He looked back to Storm and Silver. Both animals were watching in silence.

"Maybe we should wait until the magic wears off," said Elenna, tightening her grip on Tom's arm.

"We don't have time," he said. "Somewhere in that rain forest, Epos needs our help."

"You're right," said Elenna.

Letting go of his friend's arm, Tom stepped onto the bridge.

CHAPTER FOUR

CROSSING THE BRIDGE

"BE CAREFUL!" SAID ELENNA. "DON'T GO too fast."

The bridge groaned under Tom's weight. Tom's vision blurred again. He shot out a hand and steadied himself against the ropes. He managed to take another short step.

A screech made him glance up. A black shape drifted under the clouds. Tom's eyes regained focus. An eagle! It circled, suspended on the air, gliding gracefully through the red sky. It screeched again, the noise piercing Tom's brain. Was this another of Malvel's tricks? A distraction to send him plummeting to his death?

Tom gripped the ropes and inched his way across the bridge. Each time he took another step, the ropes creaked, but they held. Tom's dizziness was becoming worse. The wind was stronger now, whipping through his hair.

Shaking his head to clear his thoughts, Tom called back to Elenna. "It's safe," he shouted. The wind caught his breath and whipped it away. Had she heard him? He yelled again. "The ropes are strong enough. You can come across."

He looked around to see Elenna gingerly place a foot on the bridge. So far, so good. But as Elenna took another step, Tom realized he had made a mistake. The bridge began to lean to one side, then the other. With both of them on the bridge, plus the strong wind, the bridge was beginning to sway dangerously. Tom bent down, keeping his weight close to the wooden planks. His vision blacked out again and he heard Elenna call out.

"I have to go back, Tom. The bridge won't hold us both."

"No!" urged Tom. "You can make it, Elenna. Keep coming!"

"But I can't see!" she said.

Tom turned. He squinted and was just able to make out a blurred vision of Elenna, desperately clutching to one side of the rope bridge.

"Listen, Elenna," he shouted, as his vision faded out once more. "I need you to do exactly as I tell you. Hold the ropes on both sides of the bridge. That will steady you."

Slowly, Elenna did as he said.

"That's good," said Tom. "Now move forward. Shuffle with your feet."

Elenna was making good progress toward him, but the bridge was still swinging violently. Tom began to back toward the other side, keeping his eyes on Elenna.

"You're doing well," he said. "You're nearly at the middle."

Elenna smiled weakly, but she was still shaking with fear. Then she tripped. She thrust a hand out to break her fall, barely keeping hold of the rope with her other hand. A shudder traveled along the bridge like a wave, tilting it to one side. Tom was thrown against the ropes and cried out. He only just managed to hold on.

"Are you all right?" shouted Elenna.

"I think so!" shouted Tom. "Keep coming toward me."

Then he felt something slimy against his palm and looked more closely at the rope he was holding. What he saw made him feel sick. It was made of hair! Many different colors, all wound tightly together. Was it hair from long-dead Beasts? he wondered. Or even human hair? Who knew what evil Malvel was capable of?

The eagle screeched again, closer this time. Tom

watched its black shape swoop low over the bridge. Was this bird acting as Malvel's eyes?

Elenna had reached Tom now, and the wind had died down. They were going to make it.

"Nearly there," he said, taking her arm. Then Tom noticed the rope on his left give a tiny shudder. He looked back. The eagle was perched on the far end of the bridge. Gripping the rope between its talons, it tore at the strands with its beak.

"No!" shouted Tom.

"What is it?" said Elenna.

Tom didn't have time to answer. Before the eagle was halfway through the twine, there was a loud twang and the rope snapped.

Tom felt his feet fall away, and his whole world turned upside down. He and Elenna plunged into the air, their screams echoing through the rocky gorge.

CHAPTER FIVE

ESCAPE FROM THE GORGE

THE ROCK FACE RUSHED PAST. BUT SOON TOM felt himself begin to slow. *Of course! My shield!* he thought. Its magic was protecting him — but would it slow him enough to avoid crashing into the rocks below?

As he passed a ledge, Tom shot out a hand. Jagged rock cut into his fingers, but he held on. His whole body jarred. Elenna was falling toward him, spiraling through the air. He would get only one chance. . . .

He reached out, his fingers closing around her wrist.

"Got you!" he said. The extra weight tore at him, but he couldn't let his friend fall.

Elenna's nails dug into his hand as she clung to him. Gathering all his strength, Tom heaved Elenna onto the ledge, then pulled himself up as well. Thankfully, the evil poison that had blurred his vision seemed to be wearing off. Now he could see what he was doing.

He lay on the ground, panting for breath.

"Thanks," gasped Elenna. "You saved my life."

"How is your eyesight?" said Tom.

Elenna moved her hand in front of her face, flexing her fingers. "It's better!"

Tom gazed up. The top of the gorge was far above them.

"How can we get out?" asked Elenna.

"We'll have to climb," said Tom.

But the sides of the gulley were slick with slime. With no ropes, it would be difficult.

Tom hauled himself up against the rock face and

placed his foot in a shallow dent. Keeping his body tight against the rock, he began to pick a path upward, using the tiny crevices to lever his way.

"One step at a time," he called down to Elenna. "Slowly and carefully."

Elenna pulled herself up behind him.

As he climbed, Tom's knuckles turned white, and sweat streamed down his back. He forced himself to concentrate. *Reach. Step. Reach. Step.* Up there, somewhere, Epos the Winged Flame needed help.

The muscles in his arms and chest trembled, and his legs shook, but Tom pushed onward. Then he saw it — a rope. It was the frayed remains of the hair cord from the bridge, dangling into the abyss. Tom tugged hard on the end. It held.

"We can use this," he called down to Elenna.

He seized the rope and began to haul himself up, his feet braced against the slope. Placing hand over hand, he dragged himself up the final section of the cliff. Behind him, he could hear Elenna breathing hard. When he got to the top, Tom leaned back to help his friend up. Then they collapsed together in the dirt.

"We've made it!" Elenna gasped.

Tom turned to face the rain forest. Huge trees shot out of the earth. Their lush green leaves cast the undergrowth in shadow. He could make out vines wrapped around the tree trunks, and snaking tendrils hanging from the branches.

"Come on!" said Tom. "Let's make Aduro proud."

Tom and Elenna hurried toward the forest. Smaller trees grew at the edges, with twisted, leafless branches that seemed to reach out as they passed by. Bushes, sprouting stems lined with thorns, tore at their legs. Parts of the ground were marshy, and Tom felt squelching mud clutch at his feet. Then he noticed something strange. A patch of the long swamp grass was crushed.

He walked another few steps and saw another flattened area.

"Look, Elenna." He pointed. "They're shaped like . . ."

"Hooves," Elenna finished.

Tom nodded slowly. "But they must be ten times the size of Storm's hoofprints! What creature could have feet that large?"

Elenna didn't answer and Tom shot her a glance. She wasn't even looking at him. Her eyes, opened wide with terror, were fixed on a spot behind him. Her hand shook as she pointed.

"Skor!" she yelled.

CHAPTER SIX

AN ENEMY RETURNS

TOM FROZE. A DARK HORSE'S BODY TOWERED above him. Silver sparks flashed from its eyes. The Beast reared on muscular hind legs, churning the air with gleaming golden hooves. His mane was as black as coal, and his tail floated in the air like strands of emerald seaweed.

Skor gave a deafening roar and unfurled giant, glossy wings. Tom staggered backward into Elenna. The underside of the feathers shimmered purple like an exotic seashell, and the tips looked as if they'd been dipped in gold. Tom spotted a shimmer of emerald green in one of the golden hooves. A jewel the size of his fist was embedded there, just like the ruby in Torgor the Minotaur's ax. Skor beat his mighty wings back and forth, the draft flattening the clothes against Tom's body and blasting Elenna's hair into tangles. Then the wheeling hooves crashed back to the ground, sending tremors through the earth that knocked Tom to his knees.

Skor snorted but didn't come forward. A voice pierced the stillness.

"Very good," it said. "It is right that you should bow before me."

Tom saw a figure jump down from Skor's back. He recognized him right away. The boy was a year or two older than Tom, with pale blond hair. A bronze sword hung by his side.

"Seth!"

"That's right," said the boy. "Didn't you expect to see me again?"

Tom had met Seth once before, on a quest to free two baby dragons. But that had been another time, in another kingdom.

"How are you in —" he began.

"Gorgonia?" Seth finished the question. "I'll always be able to find you."

Tom climbed to his feet and drew his sword. "Then that makes us enemies." *I'll finish the fight this time*, he told himself.

Seth's lip curled in a sneer when he saw Tom's blade. He unsheathed his own. "I hoped I would get the chance to fight you," he said. Then he turned to Skor and pointed back into the forest with his sword.

"Begone, Skor! Do Malvel's bidding, and take care of our prisoner."

The Beast snorted and rose into the air. Then he headed back into the depths of the forest, his wing tips glittering like flames.

Tom tightened his hand around his shield's

strap. He pushed Elenna back among the foliage, whispering, "Stay out of the way." He raised his voice. "What have you done to Avantia's Beast?"

Seth laughed. "You won't see her again."

Tom clenched his teeth. "You're nothing but Malvel's puppet," he said.

"That's better than being Aduro's workhorse," Seth shot back.

Tom adjusted his grip, raised his sword, and darted forward, cutting through the air.

Seth stepped aside nimbly, grinning. "This will be easier than I thought," he said.

He lunged at Tom, who parried with a downward stroke. Seth came again, slicing an arc at Tom's legs. Tom jumped, feeling the draft of the blade pass under his feet. Seth's face became red and he hissed in anger. He brought his blade down heavily. Tom blocked upward with his shield, feeling the power of the blow shoot through his arm. Seth grunted. Tom tried to thrust underneath, but

Seth parried, and the blades jammed together. They faced each other, locked in position, faces close enough for Tom to feel the warmth of Seth's breath.

"You can't keep this up forever," said Seth through gritted teeth.

"I won't stop until it's over," said Tom, then he thrust his shield into Seth's stomach. They both toppled to the ground, but Tom was up first. "Let your sword do the talking," he said, watching as Seth climbed to his feet, his face now black with anger.

His enemy ran forward, shouting a cry, and swinging wildly with his sword. It whistled through the air, but Tom kept his shield well placed. He backed away until he saw his chance. He ducked under one of Seth's swings and twisted up behind him. With his right hand, he pinned Seth's sword arm. With his left, he held his blade to his enemy's neck.

"You've lost!" he said in Seth's ear. "Drop your sword."

Seth's blade clattered to the ground. Tom kicked it to Elenna. But as her fingers closed over the hilt, a high-pitched screech rang out through the air. It filled Tom's head and he had to let go of Seth to cover his ears. He could barely stay on his feet.

Just as abruptly, the screeching ceased. Seth was already running in the direction of the rain forest, but Tom didn't care about him anymore. He knew that the awful sound was a Beast in pain. The winged flame's feather, fixed into Tom's shield, was vibrating and glowing, and through the ruby in his belt, which helped him to understand the thoughts of Avantia's Beasts, Tom realized that time was running out for Epos.

Chapter Seven

Finding the Winged Flame

They dashed toward the rain forest. Seth had disappeared into the shadows ahead of them. But Tom couldn't follow; he had to get to Epos.

The trees were massive, the trunks taller than the towers of King Hugo's castle and some as wide as five men.

A figure appeared suddenly from behind one of the trees. Tom recognized his bald head and eye patch. It was the keeper of the gate between Avantia and Gorgonia.

"Look, Elenna!" he said. "It's Kerlo."

They watched the ragged figure hobble toward

them, supported by his wooden staff. Kerlo paused when he was still some distance away. He smiled and lifted his hand.

"Greetings, travelers!" he called out. "How fares your journey?"

"We have to rescue Epos," shouted Tom. "She's trapped in the forest."

Kerlo nodded slowly. "I warned you, did I not? Gorgonia doesn't welcome fools."

Tom felt his fists clench. "We're not fools, gatekeeper. We have a Quest to fulfill."

"The jungle holds many dangers, young one. You will need great bravery," said Kerlo. He shook his head.

Tom was tired of the gatekeeper's mocking tone. "We're not afraid of anything," he said.

"That's funny," Kerlo said. "Your father, Taladon, said the same thing to me once."

Taladon! Tom had never met his father, who had disappeared before Tom was born, but the stories of his brave deeds seemed to have reached the farthest corners of Avantia — and Gorgonia. Kerlo turned to leave.

"Wait!" said Tom. "Tell me more!"

Epos screeched again, but more faintly this time.

"Come on, Tom," said Elenna. "We don't have much time. She's losing strength."

He nodded. And when he looked back, Kerlo was gone.

They turned and plunged into the foliage.

The air in the forest was thick and heavy. It was dark, too, and the shadows shifted as though creatures were creeping through the gloom. Elenna suddenly seized Tom's arm.

"What's that?" she whispered, pointing.

Tom couldn't see anything but dense leaves.

"What?" he asked.

Elenna relaxed. "I thought I saw something . . . a pair of eyes."

Tom peered again, and felt a chill tingling his spine.

"Just stay close," he said.

The ground was covered in spongy moss, and huge fallen branches blocked the path ahead. Mysterious sounds came from all around them — shrill calls of unseen animals cutting through the air. The leaves above them rustled, but when Tom looked, he could see nothing. Somewhere in the distance a branch splintered. Tom couldn't shake the feeling that they were being watched. But Seth was nowhere to be seen.

"I wish Silver were with us," said Elenna.

Tom thought about Storm, too, and tried to ignore how heavy his heart felt without their loyal friends.

As they moved farther into the jungle, the vines became thicker. Tom drew his sword and hacked them aside. The canopy above blocked out most of the red sunlight. A black shape suddenly broke cover and shot between their heads. Tom spun around with his sword, and Elenna let out a cry.

"It's only a bat," said Tom. "It won't hurt us."

Epos's cries were fading now, but the feather in Tom's shield vibrated more strongly than ever. If they didn't find the Beast soon, perhaps they never would. Tom couldn't let that happen. *I won't let Aduro down*, he promised himself.

Then his eyes fell on a low branch. It was splintered in the center, the end hanging loose. He walked nearer. The ground was trampled, too, with a huge hoofprint.

"Skor must have come this way," he whispered. "Let's follow his tracks — they must lead to Epos."

They edged forward, keeping close together. Skor's tracks cut through the forest. Small trees had been torn from the earth, and plants trampled.

Soon they reached a clearing. Tom peered between the trees.

"Careful," he said, holding up a hand in front of Elenna. "It might be a trap."

But there she was! Epos the Winged Flame. The good Beast sat in a makeshift nest made of giant leaves. But her feathers weren't the same burnished gold that Tom remembered. They were a dirty brown. And her eyes no longer burned like molten iron. As she shifted in her nest, Tom could see that one wing wasn't folding properly. It stuck out from her body at an awkward angle. From the twisted and missing feathers, Tom could see that the bones must be broken.

"She can't fly," said Tom. "She's completely helpless."

Tears welled in Elenna's eyes. "She must be in terrible pain," she said. "Who would do something like that to such a beautiful Beast?"

Tom knew there was only one person wicked enough.

"It's Malvel's work," he said, feeling his anger rise. "And his evil helper Seth."

They broke cover and walked toward the stricken Beast. When Epos spotted them approaching, she lifted her beak and gave a soft *caw*.

"There, there," soothed Tom.

"Do you think the magical feather will be powerful enough to heal her injuries?" asked Elenna.

"I don't know," said Tom. "I've never had to heal anything this bad."

They had almost reached the nest, when a rustling came from the far side of the clearing. Tom and Elenna froze.

The leaves began to shake wildly, and tremors stirred the ground beneath their feet.

Golden hooves crashed through the foliage.

It was Skor!

CHAPTER EIGHT

FACING THE WINGED STALLION

THE BEAST BURST THROUGH THE TREES, cracking small trees like twigs. Epos lifted her head and let out a terrified squawk.

Seth ran from behind Skor, his sword held out in front of him. Tom didn't have time to draw his weapon.

Luckily, Elenna was quicker. She shoved a foot in Seth's path and sent him stumbling to the ground. He was climbing back to his feet when she swung a branch, which smashed into Seth's temple. He crumpled to the forest floor beside Epos's nest.

Tom cut down a vine and threw it to her. "Tie him up with this, Elenna!" he called.

Elenna was on Seth in a flash, and bound his wrists with the vine.

"Quickly, Tom," she shouted. "There isn't much time. The vines won't hold him for long."

A roar filled the clearing, and Tom turned to face Skor. The Beast drew back his lips. Huge teeth snapped the air.

Tom dashed away from the Winged Flame's nest. He wanted to put as much distance as possible between Skor and Epos.

He was halfway across the clearing when the winged stallion lunged at him. Tom ducked, and the Beast's stinking breath washed over him.

"Over here!" shouted Seth furiously.

Tom spun around to see that Skor's attention had turned to Elenna, who was kneeling on top of Seth. The Beast charged toward her, eyes flashing silver sparks onto the forest floor.

"Hey!" Tom shouted. "Leave her alone!"

Epos bravely tried to lift herself out of her nest

but sank back, defeated. Tom picked up a rock from the ground and took careful aim. Skor was almost on top of Elenna now, and she scrambled back from Seth, who writhed on the ground. Tom threw the rock and it hit Skor in the temple.

The Beast reared up, snorting in pain and anger. His forelegs crashed back to the ground and he charged toward Tom once more. There was no time to think, and nowhere to run. All Tom could do was roll out of the way. He found himself hidden behind a thick tree trunk.

Elenna, meanwhile, had returned to Seth's side.

"Leave him, Elenna!" Tom shouted. "You have to hide."

She looked up, and then back at Seth, uncertainty written on her face. Then she seized Tom's enemy under the armpits and began dragging him toward the edge of the clearing, away from Epos's nest.

Tom heard the crunch of Skor's hooves in the undergrowth, and flattened himself against the trunk. There was no way Tom could face this Beast on the forest floor. He wouldn't even be able to get close to Skor's head. Maybe if he could get higher . . .

Tom looked up the trunk.

Skor appeared at the side of the tree, sniffing the air. The purple feathers of his wings ruffled, and his flanks rose and fell.

Tom edged around the trunk, keeping out of the Beast's sight, then he began to climb. The bark of the tree was coarse and cracked, with plenty of handholds. Tom was as high as Skor's back when the Beast finally spotted him. The Beast's eyes opened wide, and sparks flashed against the trunk, burning the wood, then he opened his mouth and roared. Tom saw deep into the winged stallion's red throat. The huge teeth snapped at him, but Tom managed to pull his legs out of the way. He drew his sword and swung it at the Beast. It glanced off Skor's head, doing no damage at all.

"Climb higher," shouted Elenna from below. "You have to get above him."

Tom scrambled up the trunk. He reached a hollow in the trunk and climbed into it. Skor tried to unfurl his wings, but the trees were too dense here. The Beast retreated to the bottom of the tree, out of sight. For a moment, Tom felt safe.

Then the branches began to tremble, as though a strong wind were blowing through them.

"Get out, Tom!" Elenna screamed from below. Tom caught sight of her terrified face through the leaves. She was sheltering by another tree, her foot resting on Seth's back.

Then Tom realized what was happening. The Beast was tearing down the tree!

"You have to climb down!" shouted Elenna.

The Beast attacked the trunk again, and the branches where Tom was crouched shook wildly, scattering leaves below. The whole tree creaked.

Tom sheathed his sword and started to scramble

down. But it was too late. The tree leaned over, swinging wildly one way and then the other. Tom felt his stomach lurch.

A loud splintering sound echoed in the clearing, and the trunk began to topple, scything through the foliage. Green leaves blurred past Tom's face. He had only one chance. He pushed off with his feet and jumped. The ground came toward him fast.

Tom landed on the mossy carpet, bending his knees to cushion the blow, and rolled away. Behind him, the tree slammed into the forest floor. Birds shrieked and a cloud of dirt filled his eyes.

Skor was already galloping toward him through the debris. Tom drew his sword. He lifted his shield and threw himself at the golden hooves. They thudded against the wood of his shield as he swung his sword, slashing Skor's leg. The Beast took a few steps backward. Tom watched as the

cut disappeared before his eyes. The skin was unblemished again.

"A Beast that doesn't bleed?" shouted Tom in confusion. "How am I supposed to defeat it?"

"You didn't think Malvel would make it easy, did you?" Seth cackled. "Face it, you and Epos are going to die!"

"Go for the head!" shouted Elenna. "It's the only way to stop him."

As the Beast kicked out, Tom dodged sideways to avoid the blow. If reaching Skor's head was the only way to stop him and save Epos, that's what he'd have to do. *But how can I get close?* he thought desperately.

As Skor reared again, Tom saw his chance. He darted under the wheeling hooves and threw himself at Skor's rear leg, wrapping his arms around it. Skor snorted and bucked, kicking out with both his back legs. Tom felt the teeth rattle in his head, and his sword fell from his grasp.

"Tom!" cried Elenna.

His hands came loose and he was thrown through the air. He smashed into the ground among the leaves of the fallen tree, and a sharp pain stung his forehead. Blood trickled into his eye.

Skor thrashed at the ground with his hooves, then charged toward Tom, spreading his dazzling wings and lifting from the ground. As he hovered in the air, strings of saliva drooled from his jaws.

"Kill Tom!" bellowed Seth.

"Get up!" shouted Elenna.

Tom struggled to his feet and faced Skor. The Beast's wing tips scattered golden rays of light across the clearing. Tom looked around for his sword, or something else to fight back with. There was nothing. But Tom wouldn't give up. Not now — not after all they had been through.

As the Beast's hooves sliced toward his face, Tom pushed out his shield. "While there's blood in my veins," he yelled, "Malvel will never triumph!"

CHAPTER NINE

FIGHT TO THE END

SKOR'S HOOVES CRUNCHED ONTO TOM'S shield, but Tom kept his arm firm and the wood held. Then Skor whinnied in pain. Tom peered around from behind his shield and saw an arrow sticking out of Skor's flank.

"Elenna!" he cried.

His friend had left Seth's side and was walking forward toward them, stringing another arrow.

"Run, Tom!" she shouted. "I can't hold him back for long."

Tom looked around. There must be something he could do.

Elenna unleashed a second arrow, which

embedded itself under Skor's mane. The Beast backed off again, but already the first arrow had dropped out, and the skin had healed.

Tom's eyes fell on a reed-filled swamp at the edge of the clearing, and an idea formed in his head. He remembered a story his uncle had once told him about horse whisperers, people who could calm whole herds of stampeding animals by blowing through pampas grasses. Perhaps the same would work with these reeds.

Tom scrambled toward the swamp.

"Stop him!" shouted Seth.

Tom looked back and saw that Elenna was pulling another arrow from her quiver. She had only three left.

The water of the swamp was green and as thick as tar. Tom strode into the center of the reeking pond. The warm sludge swallowed his legs up to the knees. Tom tugged at the nearest reed, and stifled his cry as the sharp edge cut into his hand. He pulled again, and the reed came free.

"I've got no arrows left!" shouted Elenna.

Skor was careening toward her.

He placed the reed between his hands and blew into his palms.

A note like a shrill scream rang out across the forest clearing. Elenna dropped her bow and crouched on the floor, clutching her hands to her ears. Epos gave a cry and sank her head into the side of the nest.

Skor stopped a few paces from Elenna, then lowered his hooves. His eyes sparkled, but they no longer sent their lightning bolts into the foliage.

It's working, thought Tom. He took in a lungful of air and blew again.

Skor shook his white mane as though getting rid of a nuisance fly. Then his eyelids drooped and his green tail hung limp.

"No!" shouted Seth. "Curse you both!"

Tom gave a final blow on the reed, and Skor's head sank to his chest. He stood completely still.

"Tom," whispered Elenna. She pointed. "Your sword!"

There it was, resting at the base of a tree. Tom dropped the reed and ran to it. Holding the weapon in his hand, he approached the Beast. The mighty body towered above him. Could Skor really be asleep? The feathers in his wings didn't so much as stir.

"Be careful!" whispered Elenna.

"I'll have to climb onto his back," said Tom. "I can't reach his head from here."

"No!" shouted Seth. "Wake up, Skor!"

The Beast's eyes shot open, but Tom was quick. He threw his sword through the air with all his strength. It spiraled toward Skor, the hilt smashing into his head. The winged stallion reared on his hind legs, his mighty wings unfurled and filling the sky with their purple gleam as he cried out in pain.

But Skor's hooves did not fall back down to the ground. He remained frozen, legs raised and mouth gaping, like a statue.

"What's happening?" gasped Elenna.

A green glow began to creep up Skor's back legs. It was as though the forest were reaching out and claiming the Beast. Tom knew what was happening. He'd seen it already with Torgor the Minotaur. As green crystals began to form over the winged stallion's body, Tom leaped out of the way.

A giant emerald prison closed over the Beast. Elenna gave a low whistle of awe. Then Epos gave a warning squawk.

"Quick!" shouted Elenna. "Seth's escaping."

Tom saw Seth running away, his hands still tied behind his back. Another vine, broken in the center, trailed from his ankle. Elenna chased after him, and had almost caught their enemy when she tripped in the dirt. Seth took his chance. He dove into the shadows between the trees and was gone.

"He must have cut himself free while I was helping you," said Elenna. "I'm sorry. . . ."

"It's fine," said Tom, placing a hand on Elenna's shoulder. He stared into the forest. "Though I'm sure that's not the last we've seen of Seth."

Together they walked back to Skor.

"What's that?" said Elenna, bending down to pick up something among the long grasses. It was the large emerald from the winged stallion's hoof. "Another token for your belt, Tom."

The gemstone slipped easily into one of the remaining five notches of his belt.

"I wonder what it does?" said Tom.

A pitiful wailing interrupted them.

"Epos!" said Elenna.

The great phoenix was resting her head on the

side of the nest. Short, rasping breaths made her feathers shudder. She stared at Tom pleadingly through half-closed, glassy eyes.

"Quick," said Tom urgently. "We have to help her. She's dying!"

CHAPTER TEN

A RACE AGAINST TIME

CLOSE UP, EPOS'S WOUND LOOKED AWFUL. Forest insects were hovering over the bleeding and broken wing.

Elenna stroked the good Beast's head. "Can you help her?"

"I can try," said Tom, taking the enchanted feather from his shield. He ran it over Epos's injuries, but nothing happened. He tried again.

"Curse Malvel!" said Tom. "It's not working. Perhaps it's just not strong enough."

"Tom!" said Elenna. "Your belt!"

Tom looked down. Skor's emerald was glowing dimly.

Elenna raised her eyebrows. "Do you think . . ."

Tom pulled the crystal from his belt. "There's only one way to find out!"

He held the crystal close to Epos's wounded wing. It shone brighter the closer it came, until Tom had to shield his eyes. Soon the clearing was completely bathed in green light. Epos's wing moved a little. Tom watched in amazement. Slowly, the bones straightened out as though they were being reset by an invisible hand. Finally, new feathers appeared over the bald patch where feathers had been torn out of her skin.

"The crystal has the power to heal broken bones!" said Tom. "Even those of a Beast!"

Epos lifted her head from the nest. The life flooded back to her eyes. She opened her beak and gave a squawk of gratitude. She spread her mighty wings. A smokeless fire broke out over the feathers. Epos the Winged Flame was alive and well.

"She's more beautiful than ever," said Elenna.

With a flap of her wings, Epos sprang out of the nest and flew toward the treetops.

Tom looked up at the canopy of branches. "She won't be able to escape the forest," he said. "The trees are too dense."

But something strange happened. As Epos rose up, a slit opened up in the air in front of her. It spread until it was a circle as big as Epos herself.

"A gateway!" said Elenna, turning to Tom with wide eyes.

Tom could see blue sky. There were huge towers of stone, too, and flags fluttering on the breeze. He heard the call of distant trumpets. The smell of fresh air filled his nostrils — the smell of home.

"It's King Hugo's castle!" he said, his heart lurching. It seemed so long since he had been home. Epos was hovering by the gateway, ready to leave. At least *she* could escape the terrible kingdom of Gorgonia.

Tom and Elenna waved.

"Good-bye, Epos," Tom said. "It's time for you to see Avantia again."

The red jewel in Tom's belt glimmered, allowing him to sense the flame bird's thoughts, and he felt the warmth of Epos's farewell. He knew she was saying thank you. She called a final time, and then she flew through the hole in the sky. It closed up behind her, leaving a scattering of fiery ashes that drifted down into the clearing.

"We've done it, Tom!" said Elenna. "Another good Beast is free."

Tom nodded in the direction of Skor. "And another of Malvel's is captured," he said.

"Where do you think Seth has gone?" asked Elenna.

"I don't know," said Tom. "But we need to get back to Silver and Storm. They'll be worried."

Tom and Elenna retraced their steps. The rain forest didn't seem nearly as frightening now that Skor had been defeated.

When they reached the edge of the forest, they could see Silver and Storm waiting on the far side. Then Elenna pointed at the gorge.

"How are we going to get across? The bridge is gone!"

Tom hesitated. "What about the gift my golden boots gave me? I can leap huge distances."

Elenna frowned. "But I can't."

"I'll carry you," said Tom.

He'd never tried to use his golden boots with a passenger. If he failed, it wasn't only his own life he would be giving up. But what choice did he have?

"Climb onto my back," said Tom.

Elenna put her arms over his shoulders and jumped up. Tom could feel her heart pounding.

"Ready?" he asked.

"Ready," she replied, her voice firm.

Tom ran toward the edge of the cliff, picking up

speed until his legs burned. Then he leaped out over the gorge.

He sailed up, his feet striding through the air, and whooped in delight as the wind rushed past. The abyss opened up beneath them, but Tom wasn't afraid.

"I feel like a bird!" shouted Elenna.

The ground on the other side was approaching fast.

"Brace yourself!" Tom yelled over his shoulder. He hit the land hard, sprawling into the dirt. His shield skittered away and came to rest against a nearby bush.

Elenna was laughing. "I don't think I'll ever be afraid of heights again!" she said.

Storm galloped over and nudged at Tom with his nose. Silver licked Elenna's face excitedly. Tom brushed the earth off his knees and climbed to his feet. It was good to be back together again.

He walked over to retrieve his shield. But as he turned it over, he saw that the sea serpent's tooth in its surface was glowing and vibrating. Tom turned to his companion.

"Elenna, we have to go!" he said.

"Why?" she said, worry creasing her brow.

Tom held out the shield for her to see. "It's Sepron the Sea Serpent."

Another of Avantia's good Beasts was in danger.

"While there's blood in my veins," Tom swore, thrusting his sword to the sky, "I'll finish this Quest!"

THE SECRETS OF DROON

By Tony Abbott

Under the stairs, a magical world awaits you!

COMING SOON!

▲ SCHOLASTIC

www.scholastic.com/droon

DROON36